Coloring book

EDITORIAL FASHION

LOOKBOOK

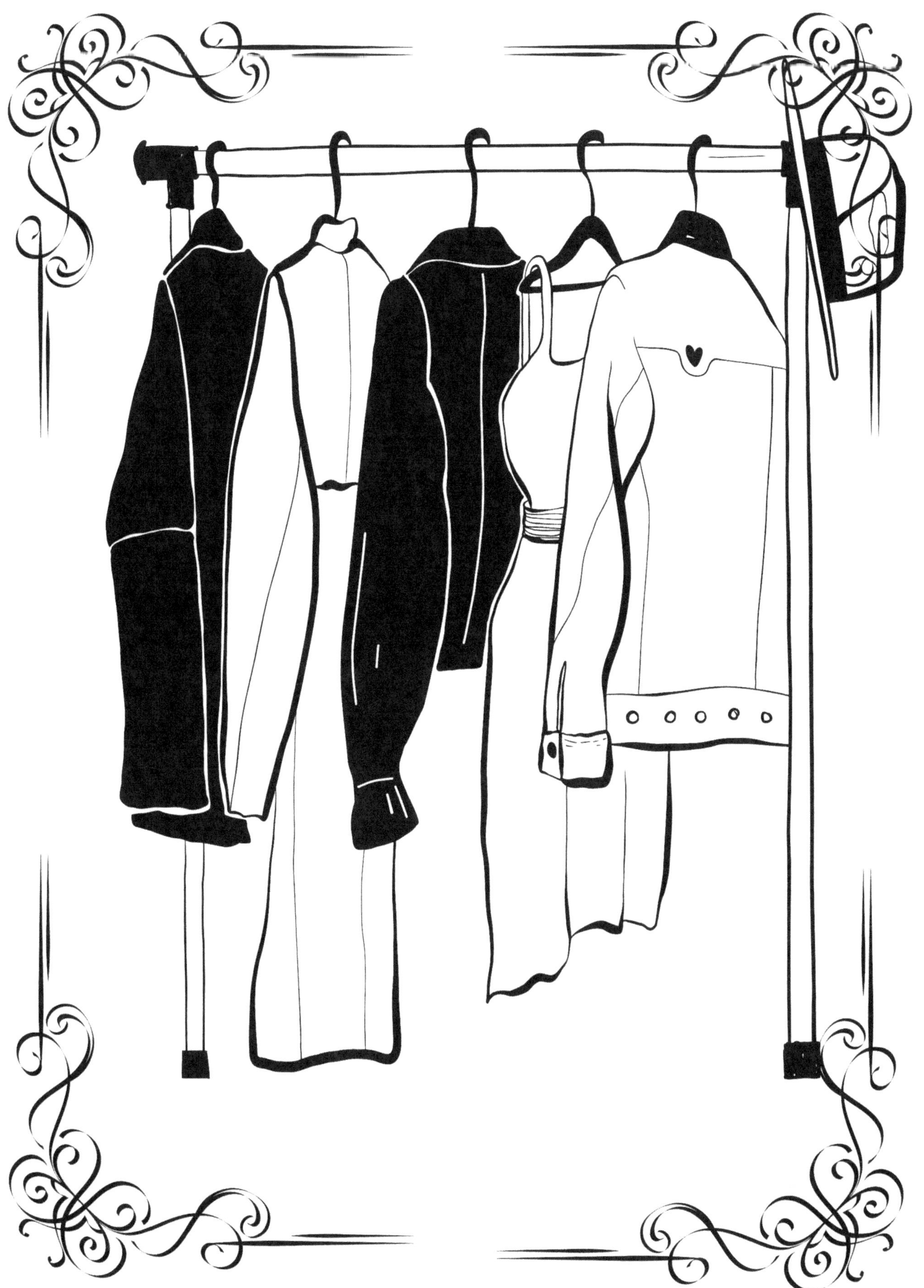

love

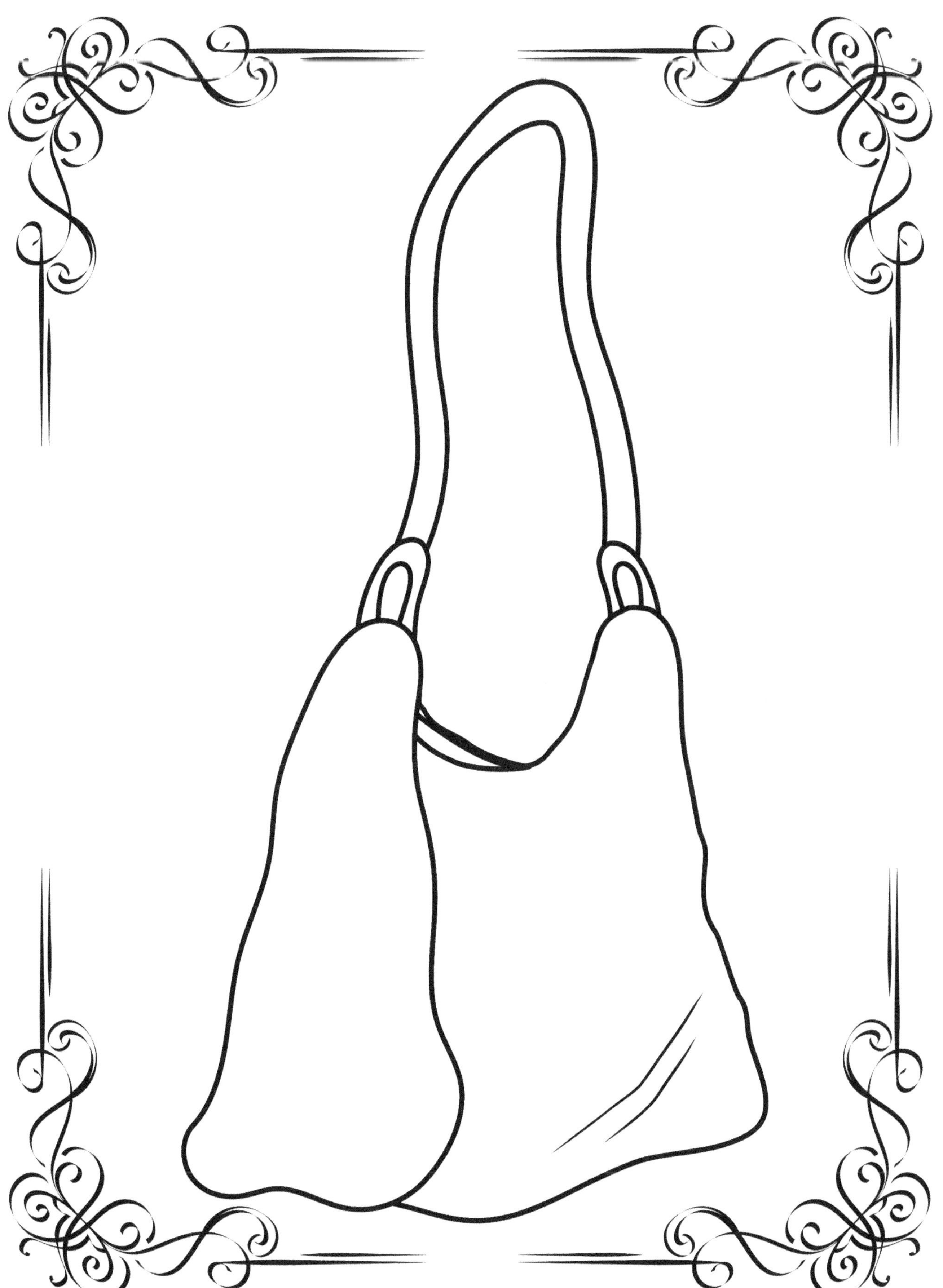

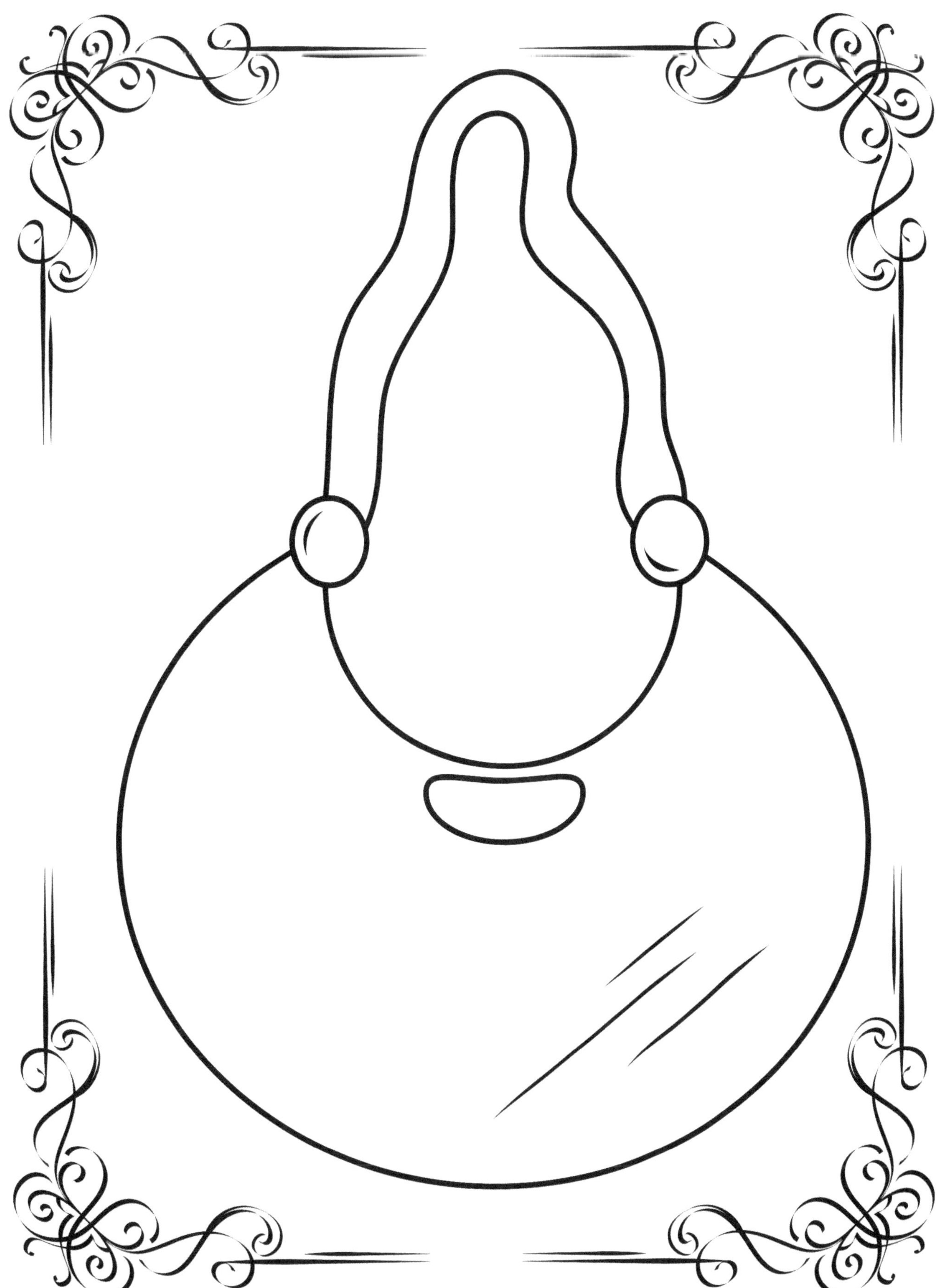

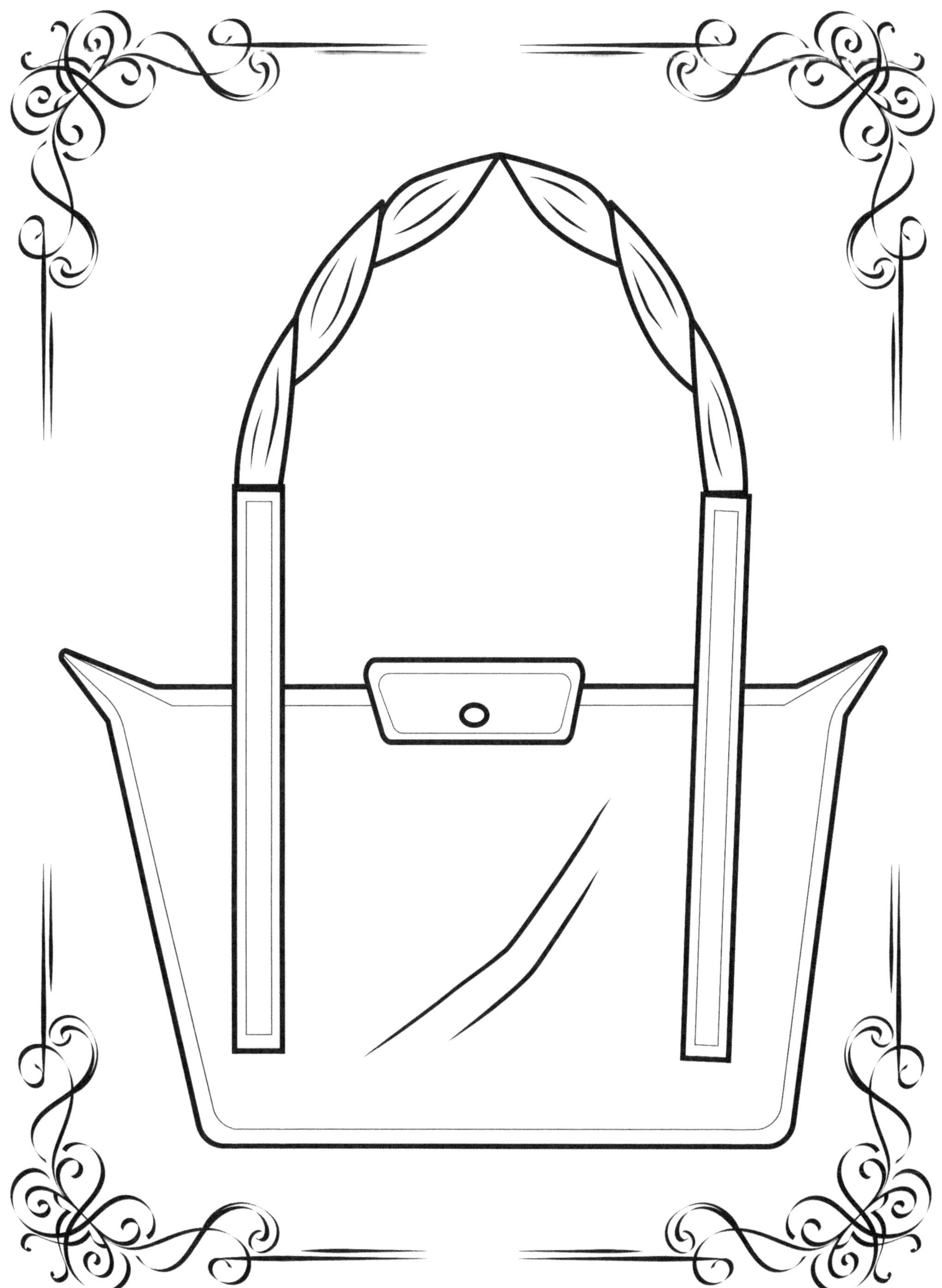

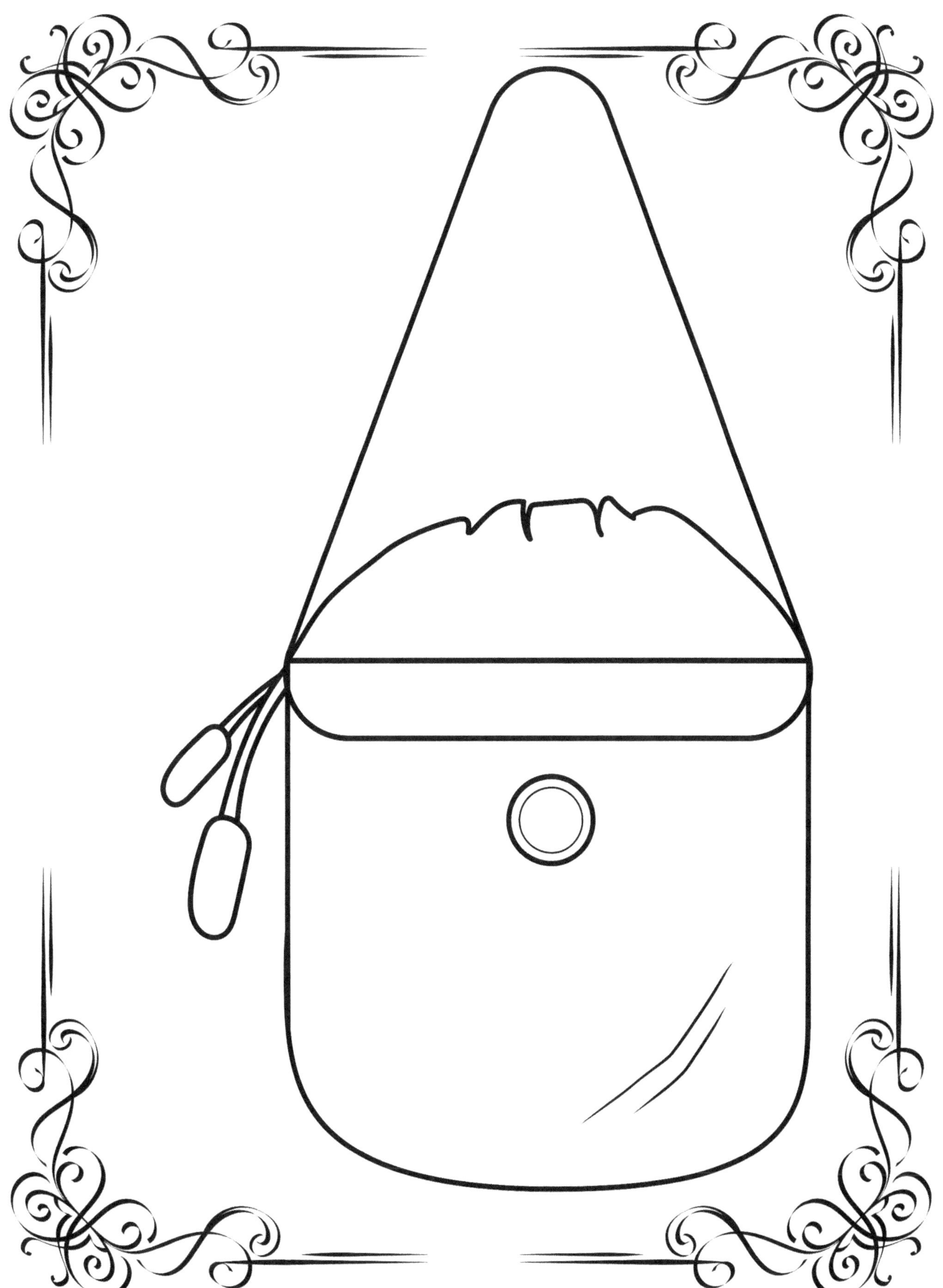

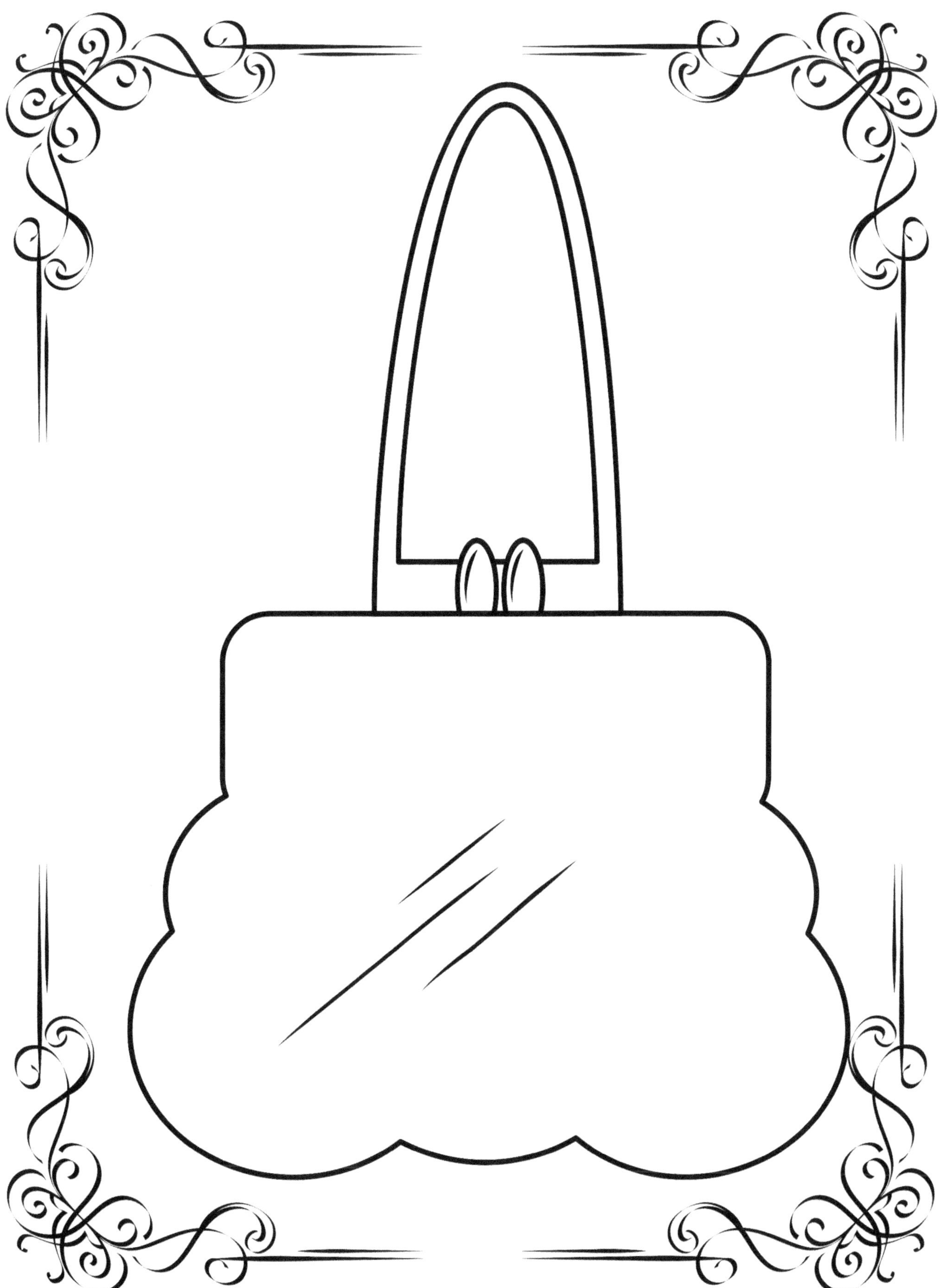

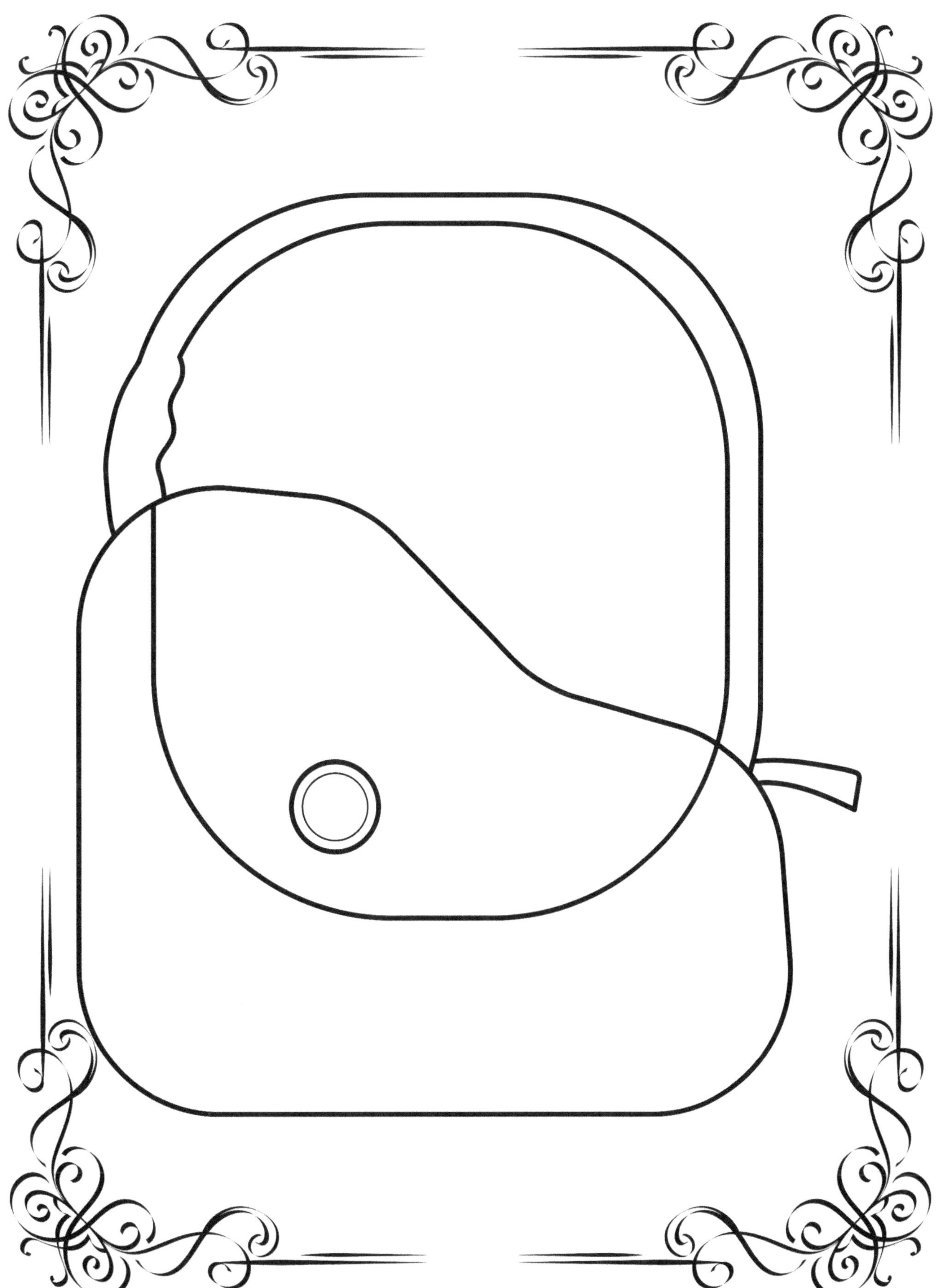

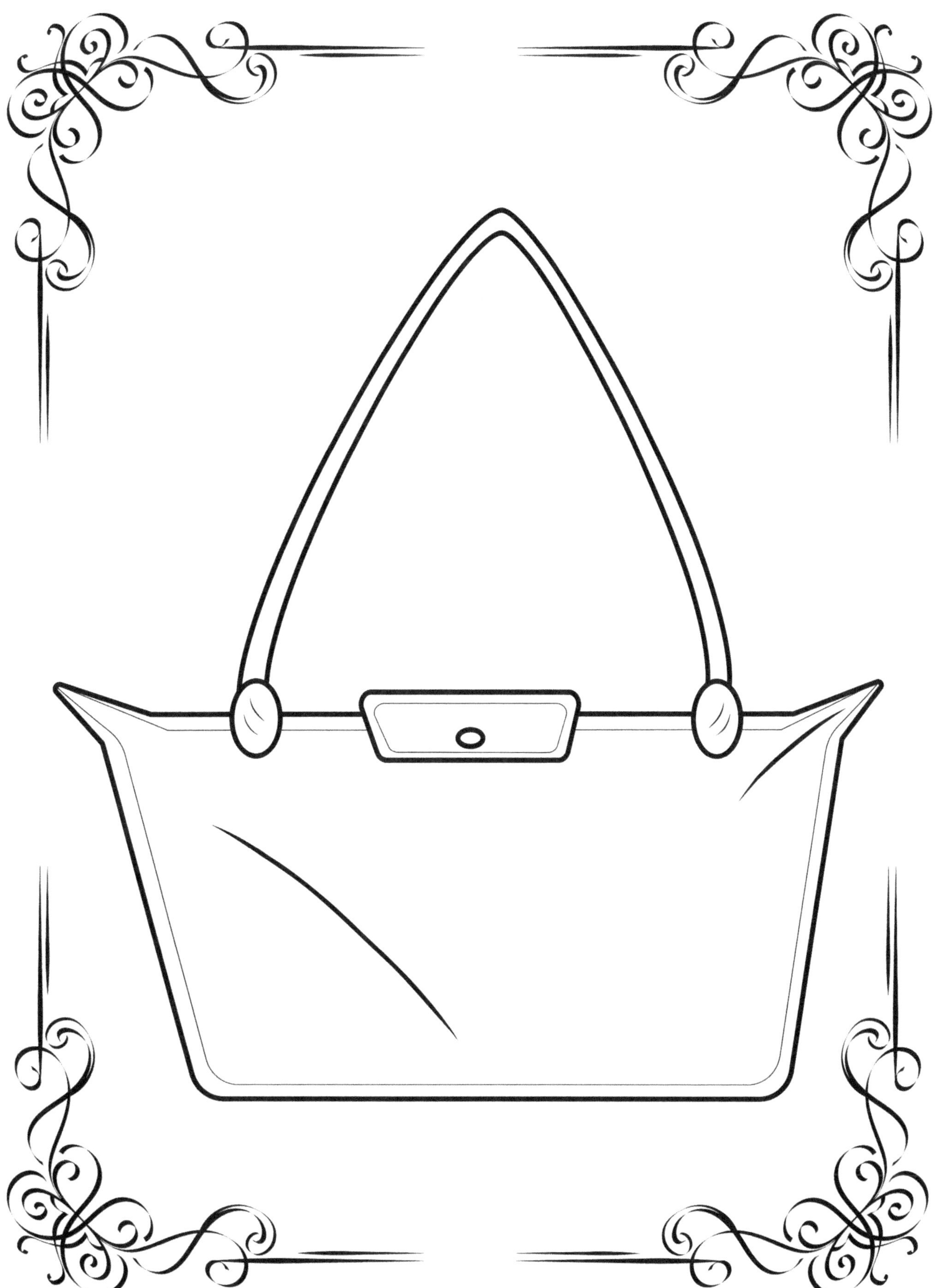

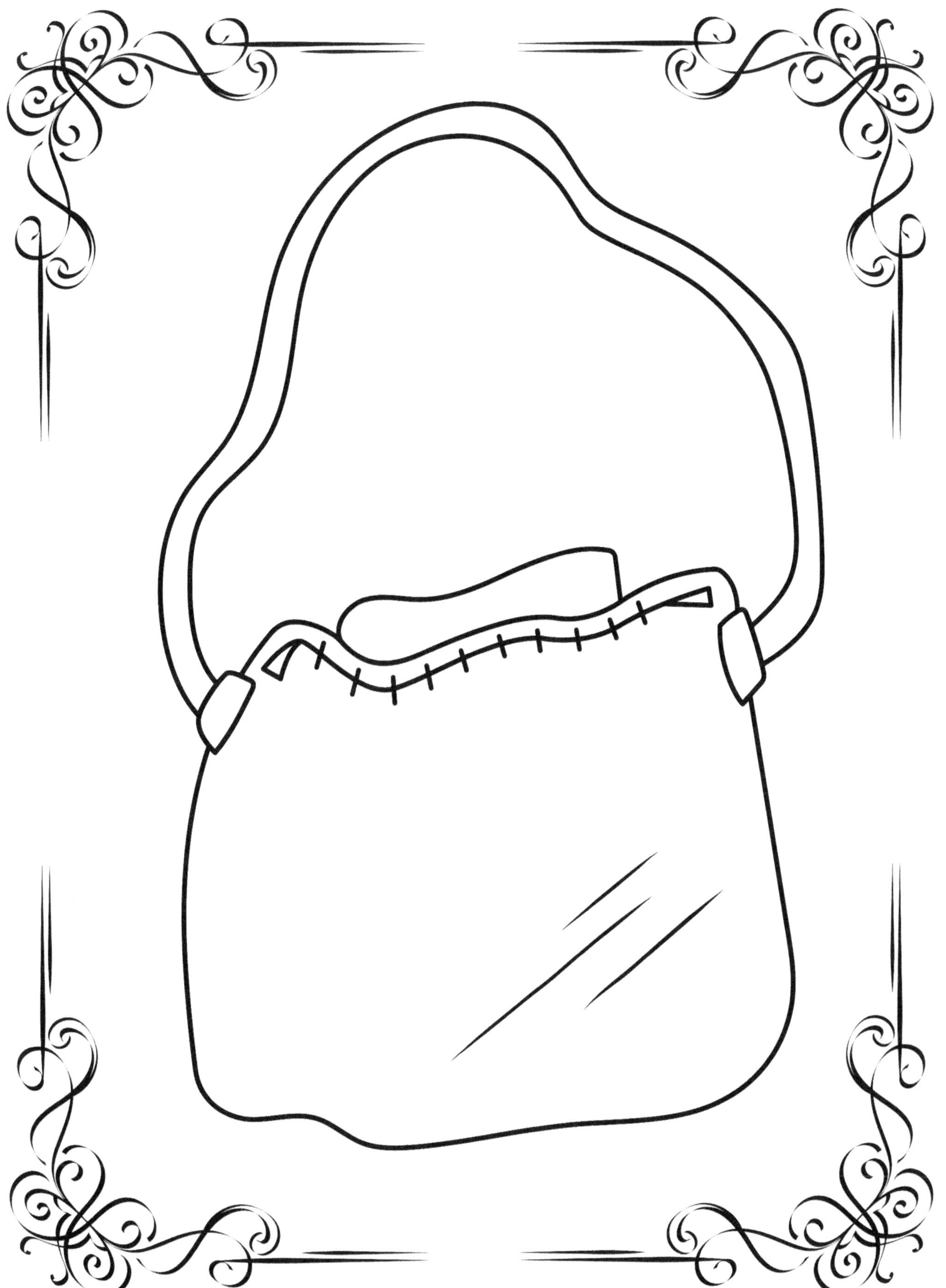

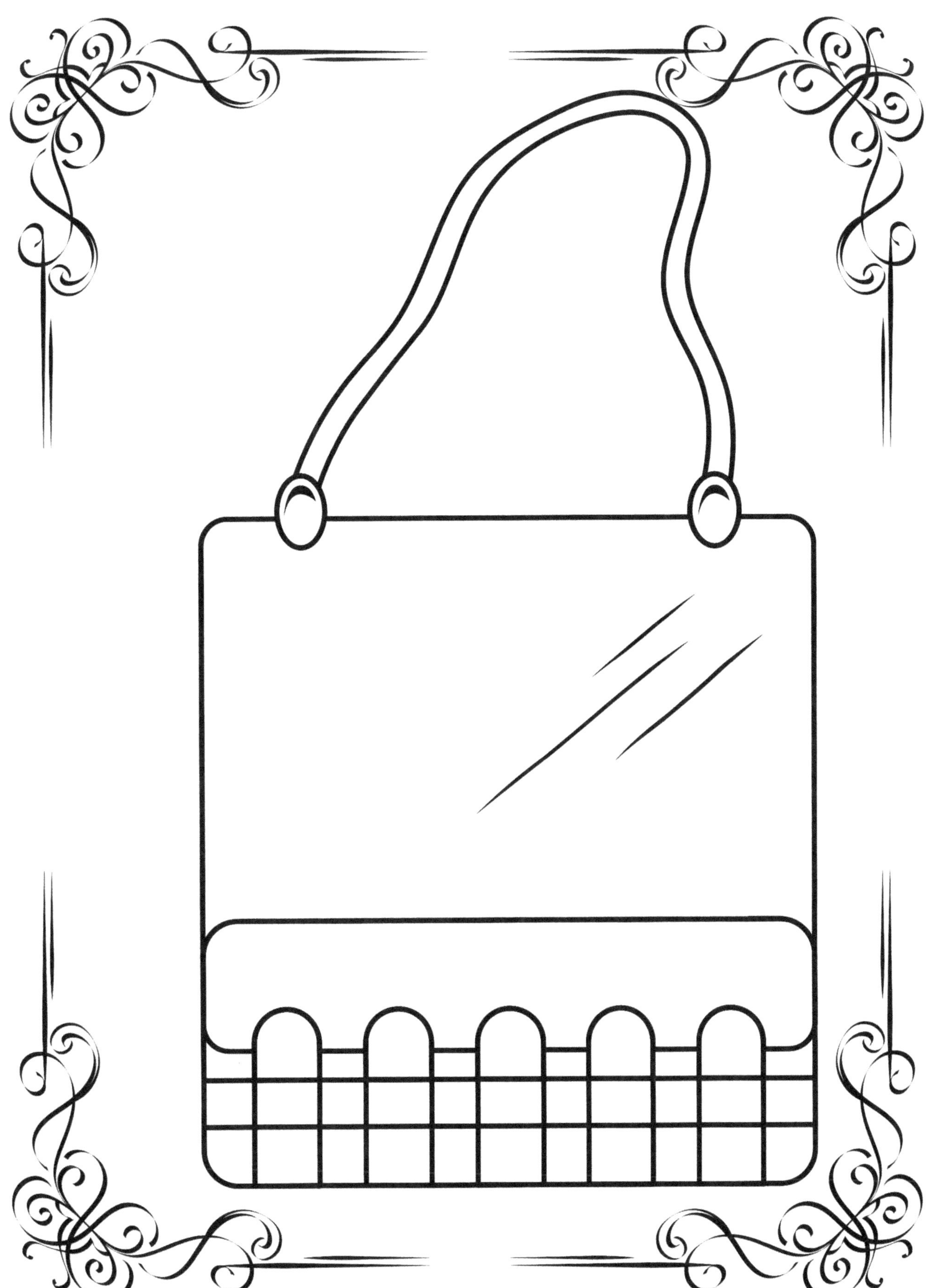

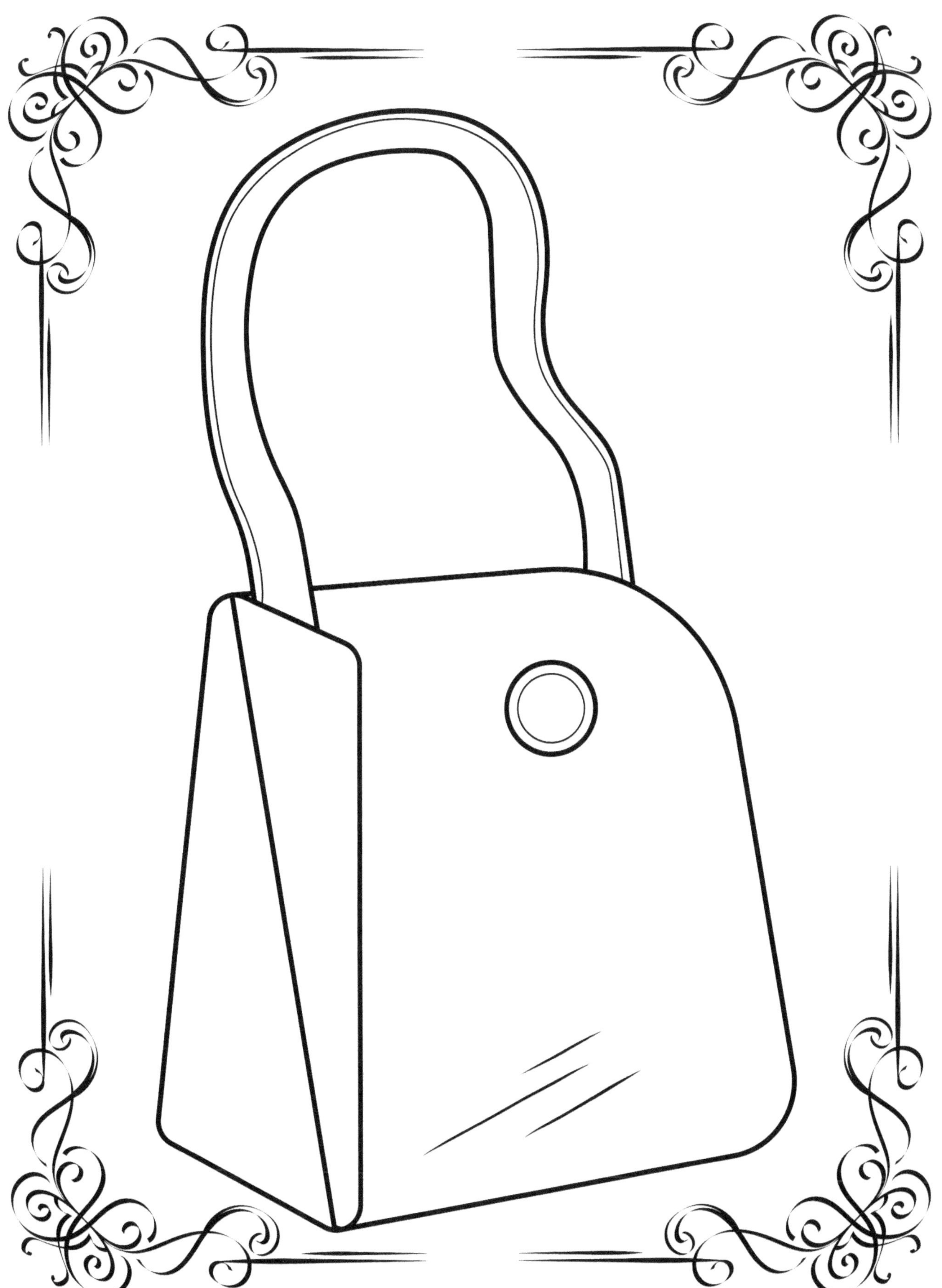

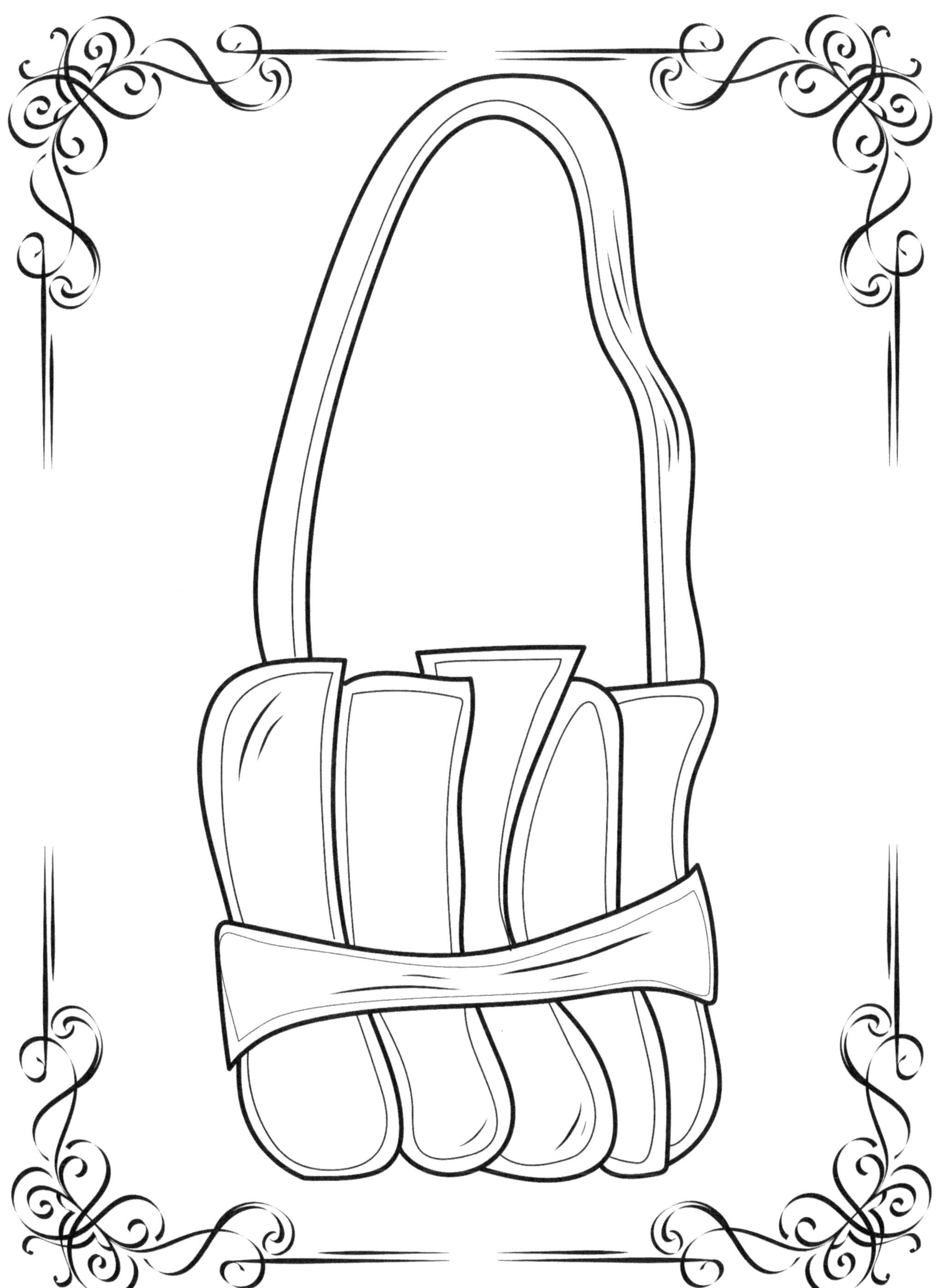

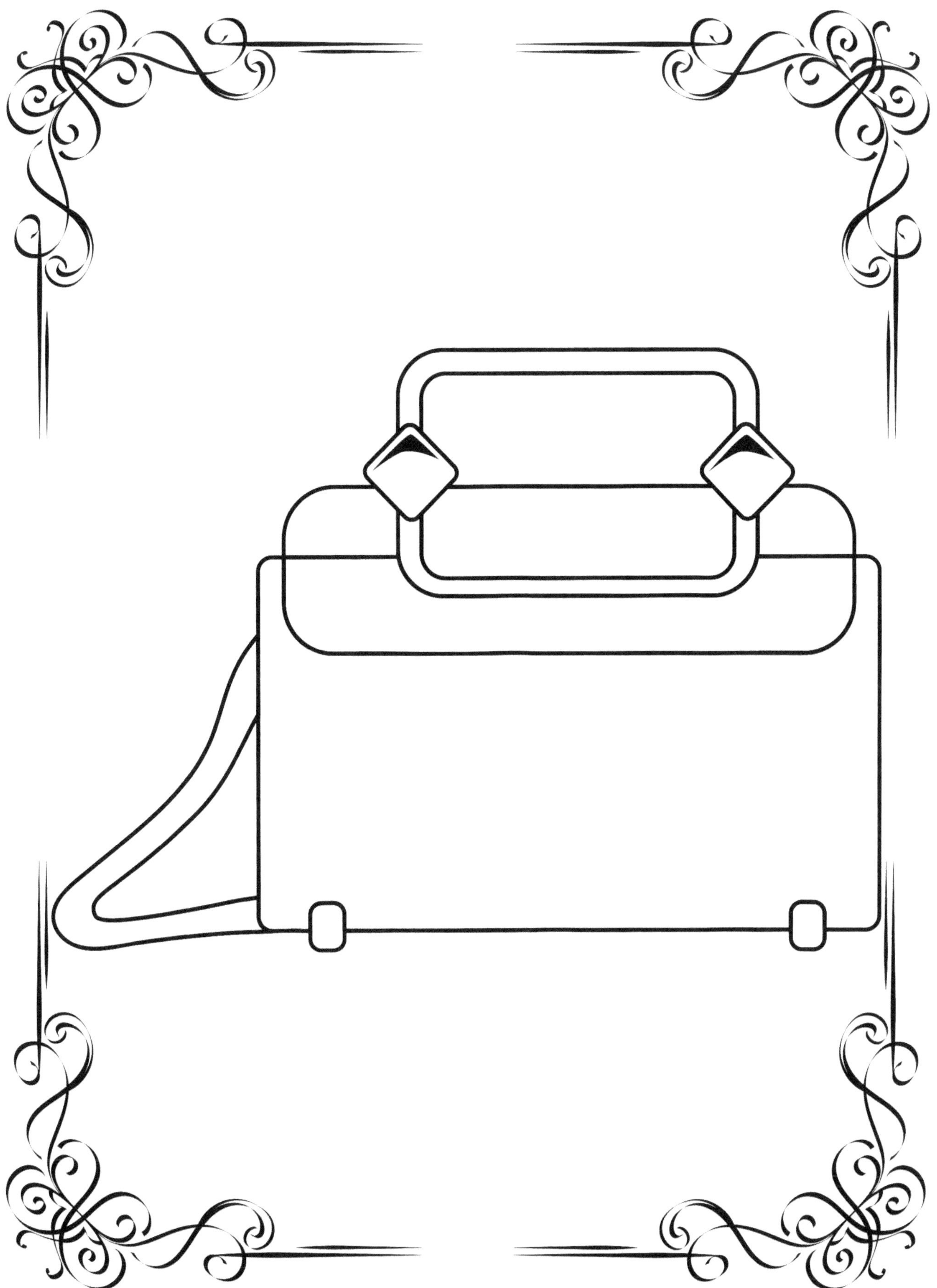

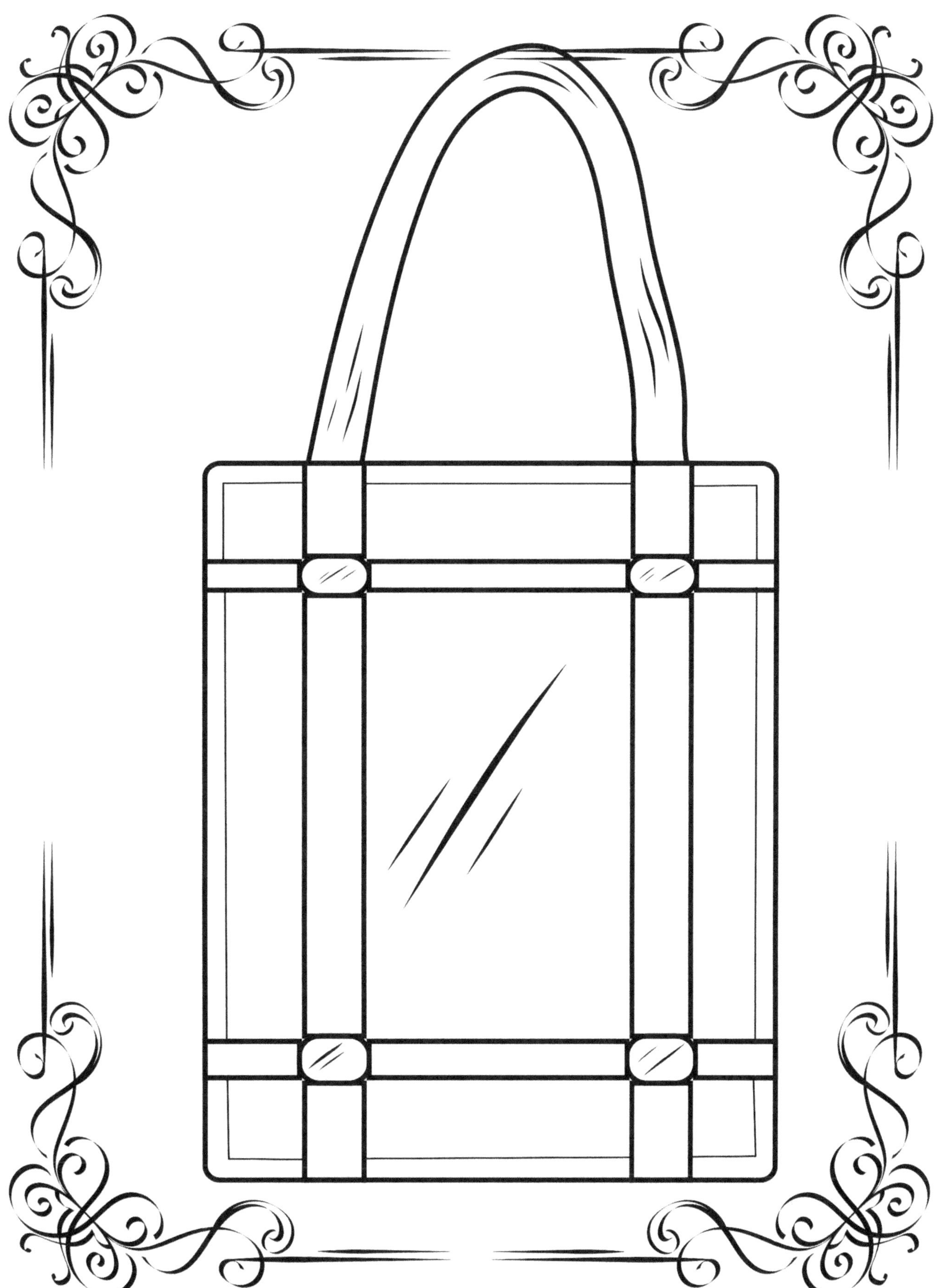

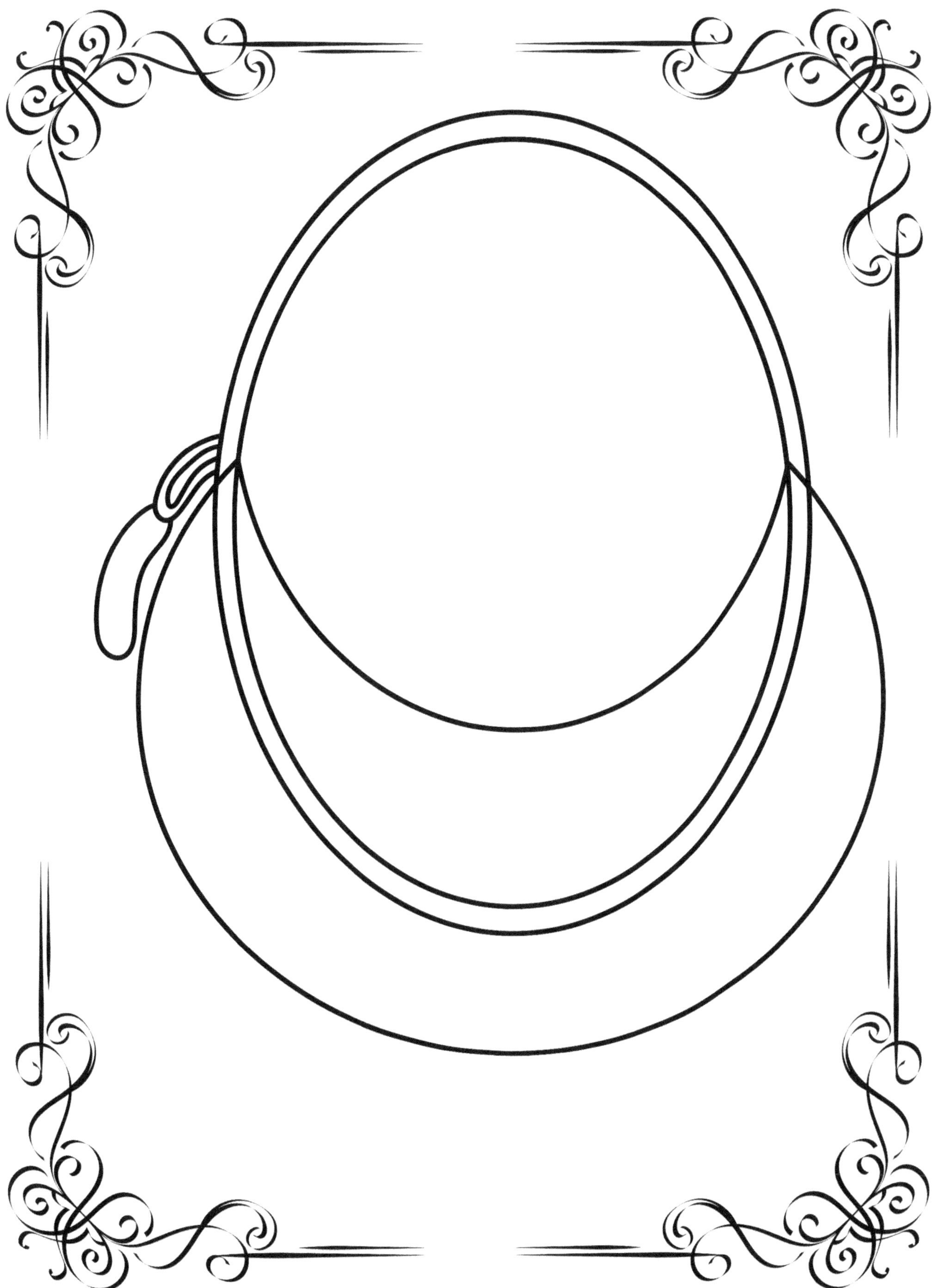

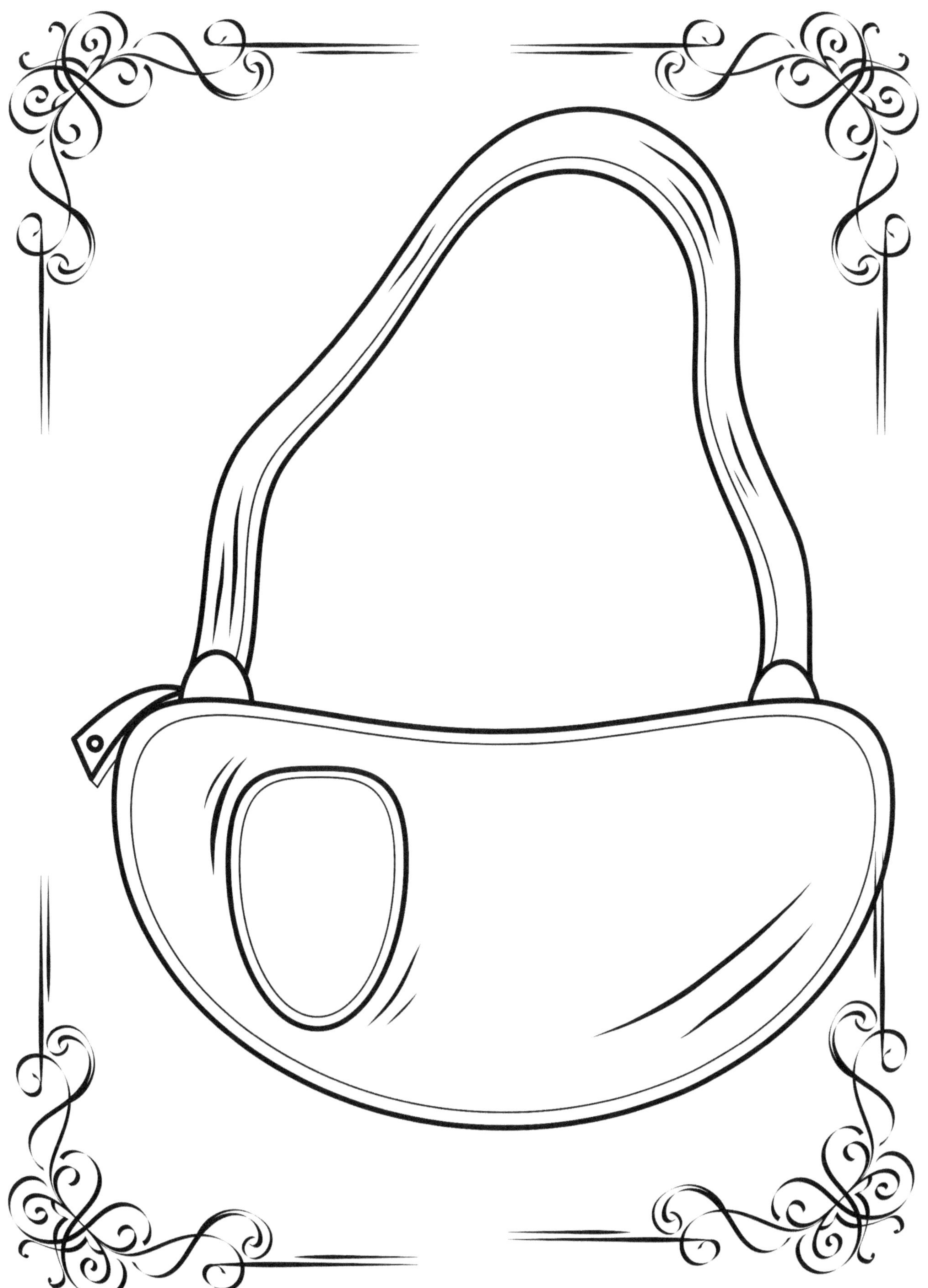